Murder at Manzanar

(Polish Dragon P. I.)

By

Steve Zimcosky

Copyright 2021

ISBN: 9798833370230

Cover Design by Andrea Ivetic Vicai.

The characters in this story were created by the author and are fictional. Any similarities to any persons, living or deceased, is simply coincidental.

Finding an Unknown

I had just finished my Tai Chi class at Cindy's martial arts school in Asia Plaza. She has come a long way since becoming the lineage holder to her father's family martial arts system. The sword still hangs in her school as a reminder of her dedication to her family and school. It was nice to get back to my lessons after the several weeks of chaos I had just gone through. Now it was time to reward myself with some delicious dim-sum from Li Wah.

It wasn't a long wait for a table and I ended up sitting at my favorite table under the television near the kitchen. Being here meant I usually got the first choice of all the little delicious delicacies rolling out on the carts. The shumai with the pork calling my name and the glistening of the light off the har gow and the pink shrimp sitting inide. The browned turnip cake, which the owner calls Chinese hash browns, is another of my favorites along with a small bowl of sticky rice. A dish made from sweet rice and filled with Chinese sausage and green onions. All served with a nice cup of Oolong tea.

Another reason why I like this table is it sits in the corner and I can see everyone who comes in and goes out. A trick I learned from my days in the Cleveland Police Department, making sure I could survey everything around me and observe who the possible malcontents might be. And to always be able to see if an attack was coming at me.

Today was not the same though, even though those little heavenly delights had always made me happy, it was not the same without my partner. I hadn't heard from Suzie in several weeks, since the death of her cousin at the cult's compound in Geauga

County. Word had gotten to me that she had taken a leave of absence from the police department and no one had heard anything more. I had no idea where she was plus there was no activity at her apartment and her mail was being held indefinitely. A tidbit I managed to get from her mailman one day while searching for her.

As I mentioned being in the corner you could see everyone coming in and out and just as I was about to put one of those tasty dumplings in my mouth I could see a woman walk in and look around as if she was searching for someone. My gut was telling me, I was the one she was looking for. It didn't take long to confirm my suspicion when she stopped the host to ask her a question and she then pointed to where I was sitting.

I sized her up pretty quickly, she had to be in her sixties with silver hair and of Asian descent. She walked like she had a purpose but I could also sense there was a kindness about her. The type of kindness you would see in a person of faith. I had seen it growing up in a Catholic family and neighborhood, the priests always trying to be kind to everyone as well as most of the nuns. There were a few that I recall didn't quite have that attribute.

She made it to my table, gave me a slight bow and asked if she could speak with me.

"What can I do for you?" I asked, placing my chopsticks down on the table.

"I am Reverend Cecilia Sangpo Abe and I am the Tokudo at the Shin Buddhist Temple and I would like to hire you, if you are available?"

"Would you like to sit down Cecilia?"

"If you don't mind, I would like to get this over with so as not to disturb your meal."

"Well, it may take a while to find out what you want to hire me for, so you might as well sit down and be comfortable. Would you like some tea?"

"Yes, I would love a cup, thank you."

I motioned for the waiter to bring me another cup as Cecilia sat down across from me. "First, if you don't mind, could you please tell me what a Tokudo is?"

She gave me a smile and said, "A Tokudo is a priest or minister if you will of a Buddhist temple. We perform the duties of the temple according to the Buddhist scriptures."

"Ah, I had no idea that there even was a Buddhist temple here in Cleveland."

"Oh yes." She was somewhat excited to talk about it. "Our temple follows the Jodo Shinshu sect also known as Shin Buddhism. We are also a member of the Buddhist Churches of America founded in 1899 in San Francisco. There are roughly sixty some temples that belong to this organization."

"Interesting. Someday perhaps you could tell me more but let's get to the reason why you are here. You wanted to hire me for something?"

"Yes, Mr. Sipowicz. Cindy, from the martial arts school, gave me your name and said that you would be able to help me. She said that you are the best person to help me with my situation."

"Cindy gave you my name?"

"Yes, she has been a member of our temple for about six months."

"I did not know that she was a Buddhist. She never mentioned it to me. I wonder why? As I recall, she and her family were Daoists."

"Perhaps, she is just exploring different faiths."

"Okay, so what is your situation?"

"I need you to find someone for me, if you can?"

"Is the person local?"

"I don't know if he is local or if he is even still alive."

She had gotten my attention with that statement, not knowing if the person was still alive could be either a challenge or as simple as finding an obituary. "What's the person's name?" I asked.

"His name is Hideki Sakura and that's all that I know."

"Why do you want me to find him?"

"Our temple was being renovated and one of the workers accidentally knocked over one of our Buddha statues and it broke open. Inside was an envelope and on it was written, in Japanese, ``Give this envelope to Hideki Sakura or his heirs.''

"What's in the envelope?"

"I don't know. It is not for me to open it. It belongs to this Hideki person or his family. That is why I want to hire you to see if you can find him or his descendants."

"There's not a lot to go on. Did you ask any of your members if they knew of him?"

"Yes, and they had never heard of him either. I am trying to contact some of the original members of the temple to see if they might know but it has been a challenge trying to locate them. They have moved away or some have passed on."

"When was the temple founded?"

"It was founded in January, 1945 by those Japanese people who were released from the Internment Camps that they were put into after the bombing of Pearl Harbor. When they were released some came to Cleveland to settle and start a new life."

"So, some of these people might know who Hideki is. Would you like me to try and find some of the original members as well? Perhaps they could shed some light on who Hideki Sakura is."

"If you would be willing to do that, I'm fine with it. We have some money saved up that may cover your fees, if not we will find a way to pay you."

"Okay, I'll take the job. Is there any way I could take a look at the envelope?"

"I have put in a safe place until he is found. I don't want anything to happen to it as it may be something very important."

"And how can I get in touch with you if I need more information?"

"You can call the Shin Buddhist Temple which is located in the old Masonic Temple on Warrensville Center Road in Shaker Heights. And here is my personal number as well."

She slid her number across the table, finished her tea, thanked me and left. Now I had something to take my mind off of Suzie. Finding a missing person could be easy or hard. I was beginning to lean towards hard as this person may not even be alive and did he leave any heirs that would be easy to find. After all this letter could have been written as far back as 1945 when the temple was first founded. I would jump right on it as soon as I finished my dim-sum.

The Search for Hideki

With my stomach now full of those tasty little treats, I headed back to my office to begin searching for this Hideki Sakura. I did a Google search but couldn't find anything but one person with that name on Facebook. After checking out the page I came to the conclusion that it was probably not the person I was looking for. This person was in Japan and from the looks of their page they had never left Japan let alone be in the United States.

A quick search for birth records, property deeds, wedding announcements and even the obituaries didn't turn up the name. Perhaps Reverend Cecilia knew something that she didn't want to share with me. But why would she do that? If she wanted this person found, why would she hold back any information? I began to ponder that question when I thought I could call in a few favors. The FBI was out since Agent Jalowiec was killed and they still hadn't found a replacement for him yet. Perhaps some of my old friends in the CPD could get me some information, and then I began to wonder if maybe this Hideki person was associated with the Yakuza, the Japanese mob.

The phone calls fizzled out; they had no information about said person nor did they have any information about any Yakuza members being in Northeast Ohio. If they did they were keeping it close to the vest because they had some sort of surveillance going on. With those channels closed I felt it was time to take a ride to Shaker Heights and visit Reverend Cecilia at the Shin Buddhist Temple.

I knew right where I was going because I had been in the neighborhood before. It was my first case when my friend from childhood,

Roger Anderson, was kidnapped by the two buffoons who thought he was a famous writer. He used a pen name, Marty McRory, when he wrote his books and they were all self-published. It was his idiot brother-in-law who managed to spout off at the bar one day while he was drunk. Talking about how Roger was worth as much as Stephen King, these two wannabe gangsters overheard him and decided they would kidnap Roger and hold him for ransom. His apartment was just a few doors down from the temple.

The temple's parking lot was adjacent to the Society bank that was right on the corner. It had been a year or so since I was in the neighborhood and they had developed the shopping center on Farnsleigh Road. It was now called the Van Aken District with upscale shops and apartments and a separate parking structure. I pulled around back where there was a door which led into the temple. There was one car there and I assumed it belonged to Reverend Cecilia.

I approached the door and it appeared like it might be locked but there was a sign that read ring the bell for service. So, I reached up with my finger and pushed the bell and it sounded like the temple bells I used to hear when I was stationed in Korea with the army. After about thirty seconds the door opened and there was Reverend Cecilia looking at me like she was confused. She opened the door and politely said, "Have you found him already?"

I gave her a quick smile and said, "No, not yet. May I come in?"

"Please do, would you mind removing your shoes please?"

It was a custom in many Asian homes and places of worship to remove your shoes before entering.

One was to leave the dirt from outside in the little area where you removed your shoes so as not to track it into the house or the temple. The other reason is that the home and the temple are considered sacred and it would be impolite to track dirt into either.

I removed my shoes and left them in the hallway that led into the interior of the building. It was a large open area that was used by whatever social club had given it up. It could have been the Freemasons but I wasn't sure and neither was Reverend Cecilia. She only knew it was donated to her group by the unidentified person who purchased it out of foreclosure. This was the area where they performed their services, whatever those might be.

She then took me on a tour of the office area and the offices that were upstairs in the front of the building. They used some for counseling and rented out to others. The front door was huge with a large, what I would call a porch, extending out toward the sidewalk. After the tour we headed back to the large open area where they performed their services. She pointed to an area just below the windows on the right and said, "That is where the statue was knocked over and broken. The letter was inside of it and we tried to find out who the person was but no one had ever heard of him."

"You said it was knocked over while doing renovations. I don't see where there was anything done here."

"No, the renovations weren't done here, they were being done in a vestibule off of the main hall. We moved it here so it wouldn't get broken."

"I see. Would it be possible for me to talk to the person who knocked the statue over?"

"He no longer works here. He quit after the statue broke, apparently he was really upset that he broke it."

"Could I get his name and phone number and address, so I could talk to him?

"Sure."

"You mentioned at the restaurant that some of the original members might have some information about who this person could be. Do you have their names and where I might be able to find them? I haven't had any luck searching on the internet nor with any of my contacts in certain law enforcement agencies."

"I can look them up, we have some of the original documents from when the temple was established, they might be listed on some of them. I can't say that they might still be alive and if they are they may not be willing to talk to you."

"Why is that?"

"Let's just say that they wouldn't trust you based on past experiences they have had with Americans in the past."

"So you're saying that they are all Japanese?"

"The original members were yes and they don't trust too many people after what happened in the 60s."

"Do you care to share that information with me?"

"Sure. Follow me and I'll share with you what I know."

She led me towards her office and offered me a seat on the sofa along the wall and some tea. Then she began to tell me the origins of the Shin Buddhist Temple in Cleveland.

The Shin Buddhist Temple was founded in 1945 by the Japanese

American Buddhists who came to Cleveland after the dismantling of the internment camps. The government called them relocation centers but they were really internment camps. It was founded on January 7th, of that year. Services were generally held in members' homes until around 1955 when the first building was dedicated on East 81st Street. A Japanese language school was started five years later.

During the Cleveland riots in 1966 members had to resume having services in their homes because the temple was firebombed during the riot. Many of the temple artifacts were stored in one person's home who tried to protect them during the riots. He managed to get them out of the temple to safety right before the temple was burned down. Everything was put into storage until a new temple was established on Euclid Avenue and East

214th Street in Euclid. That building was eventually sold and was moved into its present location on Warrensville Center Road in Shaker Heights.

She told me all of this while she was going through her files searching for names. Some of the names on the list she had told me had already passed away but there were a few who were still alive but might not remember much. Handing me the names, she suggested that she go with me to talk to them as they might feel more at ease with her there. I agreed, and I suggested she call them to let them know that we would be coming so as not to arrive unannounced. We agreed on a day and time to meet with them and I left the temple feeling that I might get some information on who Hideki was.

A Step Closer

The very next day Reverend Cecilia called and told me that she scheduled some time with the five remaining, original members of the temple. It was arranged that they would come to the temple and that I could question them there rather than making multiple trips around Northeast Ohio. One member lived in Mentor and another lived in Oberlin, while the remaining three lived in close proximity to the temple. They would be arriving there in the afternoon and she apologized for the short notice as they were all eager to talk about how the temple came about.

Since I had nothing going on I agreed to drive out and meet with the temple members. Hopefully one or more of them would have information about Hideki Sakura and I would be able to locate him and deliver the envelope to him. What was supposed to be an easy case was turning into a drawn out affair. And what if he had passed on then I would have to try and locate his heirs, which might prove to be more difficult. Nonetheless my hopes were that one of these people knew who he was and where he lived and that would be the end of it.

I arrived at the temple ten minutes before the scheduled time and parked where I had parked before. There were already several cars there and I could only assume that everyone was already here. I headed for the door and rang the buzzer and it wasn't long before Reverend Cecilia showed up to let me in. Once inside I removed my shoes and followed her to a meeting room just down the hall from her office. As we walked in everyone turned to look and there were more than five people. The reverend explained that some were unable to drive themselves so their family members brought them and she hoped that I didn't mind.

I could see the elderly members were sitting in the most comfortable chairs arranged in a semi-circle around a round coffee table. Sitting in the center was a tray with a large teapot and cups surrounding it. Cups like they have at Li Wah but maybe just a tad larger. Everyone seemed to have a cup in front of them, even the younger people who sat behind them at the table which was used for business meetings.

"Would you care for a cup of tea?" The reverend asked with a smile.

"Yes, please." I answered, smiling back at her.

As she poured the tea she began to introduce me to the elders sitting around the table, staring in a clockwise fashion. "This is Mr. Akito Egawa and next to him is Goku Haraguchi, next to him you will find Akemi Iwata, Michiko Ogawa and lastly Jomei Watanabe." They looked at me and as I was aware of protocol I bowed to them and said that I was glad to meet them. There was a chair sitting opposite them and Reverend Cecilia motioned for me to sit down and she sat down next to me.

I imagined the amount of wisdom that sat across from me at the table. Here were five Japanese elders who I was sure had seen quite a bit in their time in this country. They were all American citizens, first or second generation Japanese Americans. And I was almost certain that each of them had spent time in the relocation camps during World War II, what many people would consider a dark moment in U.S. history. After all, our government locked up American citizens, over 120,000 people rounded up and sent to approximately ten different camps mostly on the west coast of the United States. I'm sure they all had stories to tell.

Reverend Cecilia looked at me as if I should start to ask my questions and I did not hesitate.

"I would like to thank you all for coming here and giving me the time to ask you some questions. I'm not sure if Reverend Cecilia told you why you are here but I am looking to see if any of you might know a Hideki Sakura? I am trying to locate him to deliver an envelope that was discovered here at the temple. Have any of you ever heard of him?"

They all shook their heads no and I then asked if they had heard of anyone by the name Hideki or the surname Sakura. I could see that Akito was in deep thought and perhaps I had jostled something from his memories.

He looked at me and said that he remembered hearing about Matsumoto Sakura who had a trading company in Los Angeles before the war started. It was a modest size business and he would import many Japanese products to sell to the Americans and he would also send American products to Japan to be sold. Apparently Matsumoto had been sent to the Manzanar Camp in California, and he had heard about this through the first minister of the temple, Seiichi Masamune. He was in the camp with Matsumoto.

"Can you remember anything else about Mr. Sakura?" I asked.

"Yes, Reverend Masamune said that Mr. Sakura had five Buddhist Statues that he would give to five Buddhist ministers who were in the camp and one was to Reverend Masamune. He managed to get them into the camp because they were only about two feet tall and he hid them in his luggage."

"Did Reverend Masamune mention anything about Hideki Sakura?" I asked.

"No, although he did say that there was a terrible event that happened at the camp and the entire Sakura family was killed in a fire in their building. After the fire was put out the bodies were so badly burned they couldn't identify them. It was quite a tragedy, he said."

"Reverend Masamune did not mention any of the family member's names?"

"No, he only talked to Matsumoto who was a devout Buddhist and they talked much about the teachings of the Buddha. Although the reverend did say that he felt like Matsumoto felt like he was being watched."

"Watched by who?" I asked. "Did he happen to give any names?"

"No names but he suspected one of the guards at the camp was watching him and his family. Which is probably why he didn't talk about them much. He was trying to keep them safe perhaps."

"Apparently that didn't work because they died in the fire anyway." I said, wondering if there was more to the story.

"Did the Reverend Masamune say where the other statues had gone to?"

"He said they had gone to four other ministers who were at the camp and when they were released they had gone back to the temples they had been a part of before being confined in the camp. One was in Phoenix, Az., Chicago, Il., New York, N.Y., and

Seattle, Wa., and the last one was here in Cleveland."

"Do any of you know if the statues are still there in the temples?"

Akemi Iwata spoke up, "We had heard that the other statues had been broken by thieves trying to steal them. And the ministers were killed in the act of the robberies. They all happened at different times but we never heard of anything being inside of them."

My thoughts were to now contact the other temples to see if there was anything stashed in their statues. It would be kind of awkward to ask them about it since they had been broken during a robbery and the murder of the minister. Something was telling me there was more to the story than this. I had that feeling in my gut again and it hasn't failed me yet.

"Reverend Cecilia, would it be possible for me to contact those other temples and talk to them about what may have happened?"

"I don't see why not but let me contact them first to see if they are okay with it. I will contact you as soon as I know something."

"That sounds good." I looked around at the elders who were sitting there and I asked, "I know this may be presumptuous on my part but would it be possible for you to tell me about your time in the internment camps? I am curious as to how you were treated and what life was like living there."

They looked at each other and smiled, it seemed like they were willing to share those memories with anyone who would listen and I was one who was enamored by how these people had been treated. Besides I had gotten some information about the Sakura family and I could check with an old army buddy to see what he could dig up for me.

Life in Internment

Michiko Ogawa was the first to talk about her time in the internment camp. She was in the one at Tule Lake in California where Jomei Watanbe was as well. Besides those two the other three were at camps called Gila River in Arizona, Poston in Arizona and Heart Mountain in Wyoming and that was only four of the ten camps that had been established by the War Relocation Authority. It was created in 1942 by President Franklin Delano Roosevelt and it gave the army the authority to create a military zone and to remove all residents of Japanese ancestry and put them into one of the ten camps.

The camps were built under the direction of Milton Eisenhower and Dillon S. Myer, who would later be in charge of the Native American Relocation Program that would try to assimilate the Native Americans into society. Some of the Japanese were separated based on a controversial loyalty program where they would be assisted in finding jobs and housing outside of the camps. Those deemed disloyal were treated more harshly and sent to stockades at the camps. And let's not forget that these were American Citizens, first and second generation Japanese Americans.

All five seemed to describe the same kind of conditions at the camps. The camps were divided into blocks that could number anywhere from 40 to 60 and were inhabited by residents anywhere from 250 people to 300. Each block was managed by a mayor and council elected by the residents, but didn't have much real authority, to maintain orderly life. Each block had a mess hall and the food was rationed by the government and was not very appetizing. A co-op store was available generally in the middle of the compound to purchase hygiene needs, drugs and candies.

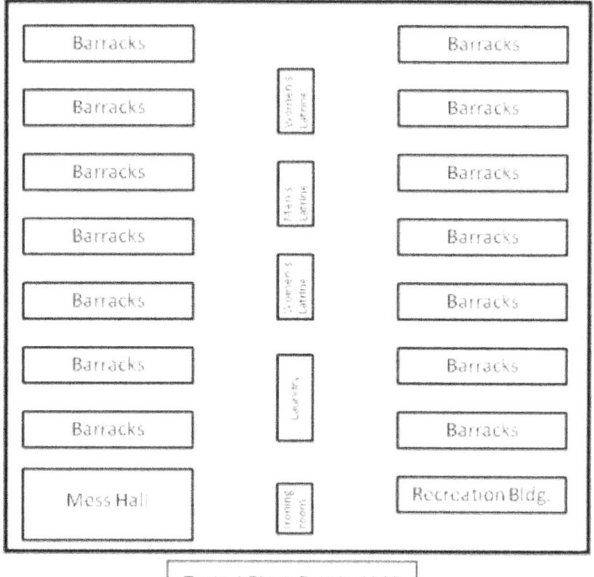

Typical Block Built in 1942

(From the National Park Service)

The barrack style housing held two to three families, in apartment style housing, with no more than twenty to a barracks. The walls usually did not reach the ceiling and each apartment was about twenty feet by twenty four. Each block had about fourteen barracks along with a laundry facility, male and female latrines and an ironing room. Residents ate in a mess hall and there was also a building for recreation.

There was very little privacy, no plumbing, or cooking facilities and there was only one light that hung from the ceiling in each apartment. All beds were single beds and very uncomfortable

Each camp included schools, post offices, hospitals and warehouses, which were not the greatest by any means. The schools were inadequate because there were not enough people to teach and classes were too big. The warehouses were not very well attended and a lot of the internee's possessions were either destroyed or stolen.

Visitations were limited only to family members, who served in the armed forces, and roll calls were done in the morning and the evenings to make sure no one would have escaped. Each person was given an identity number which is what was used for the roll call. They wouldn't even use their given names. Many found solace in religion; both Christian and Buddhist services were available and held regularly.

Self-improvement classes were available and they ranged from American history to vocational courses such as secretarial and bookkeeping skills. The younger people spent time dancing and playing sports and most classes were listed in the camp newspaper. All of this taking place behind barbed wire fences and military guard towers and patrols.

All of this continued until January 2nd, 1945 when the internment was over and the Japanese were allowed to leave the camps. But life would not be normal for many of them. They were forced to give up their belongings before entering the camps and forced to sell their homes which many European Americans purchased well under the value of the home. Those who owned businesses were forced to sell them or close them. Many of them weren't even welcomed back to their original neighborhoods.

Some of them moved to new cities via the War Relocation Authority who received job notices from employers willing to hire the Japanese Americans. It was how many found their way to Cleveland and settled in the areas of Hough and Glenville. Most who came to Cleveland found the community generally receptive to them. They never attempted to build a "Little Tokyo" because the official policy of the WRA was to spread the families out to avoid creating targets. These five elders were some of the initial families who moved to Cleveland to start their lives over.

In 1988 The Civil Liberties Act was signed into law by Ronald Regan and those incarcerated were given letters of apology from the president and token reparations. The fund also created an education and research fund. It was still a blemish on how the United States treated American citizens without any due process that is guaranteed under the fifth amendment of the U. S. Constitution.

Murder in the Temples

The next day Reverend Cecilia called to let me know the ministers of the other four temples where the statues were destroyed were more than willing to talk to me. She had set up a time for a group call and wanted to know if I could be at the temple around one o'clock. Without hesitating I agreed to be there. It more than likely was just some thugs looking to score money by stealing artifacts from the temple. I would also be interested to know if there was anything stolen from local churches and synagogues near the temples.

I did my usual morning workout to make sure I was in shape and ready for any possible confrontation I would encounter and then headed off to the office to check on emails and phone messages, before heading up to the temple. It wasn't unusual for me to get a few simple cases that I could handle in between lulls I found myself in on larger cases. My eyes couldn't believe what I was seeing in my inbox for my emails. It was an email from Suzie letting me know she would be in town for a few days and would contact me when she arrived.

There was no phone number for me to call her back and I knew if I sent her an email she wouldn't answer it. She had her mind made up and there was no getting ahold of her if she didn't want to be found. I could only wait until she arrived and contacted me.

I grabbed a quick bite to eat and headed north to Shaker Heights to meet Reverend Cecilia at the temple. There wasn't too much traffic and I made it there in about thirty minutes. Parking in the back as I had become accustomed to, I made my way to the door and rang the bell. Reverend

Cecilia let me and we headed to her office to wait for the conference call to begin. The ministers who were participating were Reverend Izumi from Phoenix, Reverend Ken from Chicago, Reverend Joe from New York, and Reverend Ron from Seattle.

There was a glitch with the phone system and we started fifteen minutes later than we were supposed to. Cecilia introduced everyone and opened it up for me to ask questions. My first question was, "Can you tell me the Buddha statue was destroyed and anything else pertaining to the robbery?"

Reverend Izumi spoke up first. "It was back in 1965 when someone broke into the temple and tried to steal the Buddha statue that was given to us as a gift. The minister at the time lived next door to the temple and saw there was a light on after hours and went inside to find out what was going on.

He apparently startled the burglar, who dropped the statue and for some reason decided to shoot the reverend."

"I'm sure the police conducted an investigation, could you tell me what they found?"

"They said it was probably someone looking for something to steal and sell to get money for drugs. No one was ever caught and we just forgot about it until Reverend Cecilia called and said you wanted to ask us some questions."

Reverend Ron was the next speaker. "Yes, it was pretty much the same thing here in Seattle. A robber broke in, we assume to steal the statue and our minister was shot dead as well. We were given the same reason, someone looking for quick cash for drugs and no one was arrested either. It seemed like the person who committed the crime disappeared."

'Was there no evidence found at the scene?" I asked.

"No, there were no fingerprints or anything left behind that could be used to locate the killer. Of course there was no DNA testing available back then."

"When did you say this happened?"

"It happened in 1968."

Reverend Izumu chimed in as well. "It happened here in Phoenix in 1965."

Reverend Ken and Reverend Joe jumped in as well. "It happened here in Chicago in 1970." And Reverend Joe said it happened in 1972.

As I sat there listening it didn't seem like there was a pattern each break in and killing took place two to three years apart. Although Reverend Joe mentioned that the minister at the time in New York was stabbed to death and Reverend Ken said the minister in Chicago was strangled to death. Of course no fingerprints were left behind and no trace of the killers. It struck me as odd that there was no evidence and it made me think that perhaps it was a professional.

I made my thoughts known to the ministers on the call and they all thought that it was impossible. Why would anyone want to kill those ministers? They all felt it was just a robbery gone wrong. But it made no sense to me. A low life druggy trying to steal something for cash would have definitely left some sort of evidence behind. Most definitely fingerprints as they probably wouldn't even be thinking of wearing gloves to hide the fact they were there.

Suddenly it dawned on me that these four other temples were given one of the five statues from Mr.

Sakura. Could the statues have some sort of part in all of this? What if the envelope that was left in the statue here in Cleveland was what the person or persons was looking for? Could it be what was left for Hideki Sakura may have something to do with this?

"Gentlemen, would it be possible for you to email me anything that you might remember later on? And also if possible any police reports that may have been shared with the temple at the time?"

They all agreed and when the call ended I looked over at Reverend Cecilia. She could tell something was up by the look on my face.

"What is it?" she asked.

"What if the ministers who were killed were done so on purpose?"

"Why would anyone want to murder a Buddhist minister?"

"Perhaps to find what was in the statue. Four of the temples robbed were temples where Mr. Sakura had given them the statues of the Buddha. What if the killer was looking for the envelope that was found in the statue here in your temple?"

I could see she was now beginning to think that it could be a possibility. After all, no other Buddhist temple was robbed or the minister killed at any other time. It just seemed to be the ones where the statues were located. If that was the case, then what was so important about that envelope? We needed to see what was in the envelope but she refused to open it until the rightful owner was found. And that would mean locating Hideki Sakura or one of his descendants.

Tragedy in the Camp

Through all of this I had gotten a lead on where to look for Hideki Sakura. Akito Egawa, one of the original members of the Cleveland Buddhist Temple, remembered that the first minister of the temple had known of a Matsumoto Sekura who was in the Manzanar Internment Camp, located in California. I had an old army buddy from my days in the service who might be able to help me out. He ended up being a lifer and spent all of his time in the army. The last I heard he had finally risen up in the ranks to a lieutenant colonel. A quick search of his name would surely give me his current deployment status.

My search showed that Scott Ramsey had now reached the rank of Lieutenant Colonel and was stationed in Washington D. C. and worked at the Army Center of Military History. It didn't quite show in what capacity he worked but a quick call to the main number and I was sure I would be able to get in touch with him in no time. After about forty-five minutes I was finally able to get him on the phone.

"May I speak with Lt. Colonel Scott Ramsey, please?"

"This is Colonel Ramsey, who am I speaking to?"

"The person you owe your career to, that's who!"

There was a pause on the other end when his voice finally came back, "Tom Sipowicz, you son-of-a-bitch, how the hell are you?"

"I'm doing well Colonel, how about you? I see you finally made it to the upper ranks."

"It took me some time but yes, I finally made it."

"Got you a nice cushy assignment in D. C. huh?"

"It'll do. How long has it been Tom? When was the last time we saw each other?"

"About ten years ago when you were still a captain. You were passing through Cleveland and we met up for a couple of drinks."

"Wow, it's been that long? And what do you mean I owe my career to you?"

"Well, I could've busted you back in Korea for looting that temple and taking a lot of those religious items. Chances are you would have been dishonorably discharged if I hadn't convinced you to give them back. It would have created a nightmare for the army and the Korean Government but you were so drunk you didn't even remember doing it."

"Oh man, I completely forgot about that. I was so glad you managed to smooth things over with the head of the temple. I really owe you one."

"I'm glad you agreed to do some free work to help atone for what you did. Anyway, I need to cash in on that favor you owe me."

"Ah, so that's why you called. What can I do for you?"

"I need your help in finding out what happened to a Japanese family who was sent to one of the internment camps back in the forties. Can you do it?"

"I'm not sure. I mean, I know that this is the Army Center for Military History but I don't know if that information is here. What's this about?"

"I'm trying to locate the person's heirs and I'm not having

much luck finding him through the internet. Plus it might involve some murders of some Buddhist priests."

"Give me the information and I will see what I can do for you Tom. It might take several days but I will let you know one way or the other."

I told him who I was looking for and gave him all of the information that I had obtained from the elders at the Cleveland Temple. If anyone could get the information for me it would be Scott. In the meantime I would keep searching to see what else I could dig up. The impulse to call the cities where the Tokudos were murdered, was an idea that could shed some light on the importance of the statues.

As it turned out not much information was readily available as the cases were so old, and the files were stored in a warehouse somewhere, if they still existed at all.

Not like today's files that are stored in the cloud somewhere. Nonetheless I had to try. Some of the detectives agreed to call if they found out anything new but I knew I would probably never hear from them.

After several days of banging my head on the computer my old buddy Colonel Ramsey called to let me know what he found out. "Hey Tom, I was able to dig up some information about what you asked and it wasn't easy. That's a subject many people don't want to talk about."

"Yeah, I know. What were you able to find out?"

"Well there was a Matsumoto Sakura who was at the Manzanar camp with his family. He had a wife and three kids, two boys and a girl and one of the son's names was Hideki. Unfortunately they had all died in a fire in their barracks back in 1943. The neighbors alerted the guards to the fire but by the time they got there to put it out the bodies were very badly burned."

"Were there any witnesses? Did any of the neighbors say anything?"

"If they did see anything they weren't saying anything. After all they felt like prisoners and who would listen to them anyway. Remember no one trusted the Japanese back then. And the bodies were just buried in a grave in the camp."

"Okay, thanks Scott. I appreciate you taking the time to do this for me. Let's get together a little sooner next time Okay?"

"Yeah, but before you go there's one more thing you should know. I found out that the army was keeping a close eye on Mr. Sakura. They thought he was an actual spy and passing on information to the Japanese through his business."

"What type of business?"

"Apparently he had some sort of import/export business with direct ties to Japan. They felt he was sending information about cities and the layout of California in his shipments back to Japan. It was thought that he hid them in some of the statues that he was shipping back. Of course nothing was ever found or proven."

"Thanks again Scott. Maybe I'll come to D. C. and you can give me a tour."

"Will do buddy, take care."

As he hung up I couldn't believe what he had just said. Was Matsumoto Sakura a spy? Was the document found in the statue some sort of information that was to be delivered to the Japanese during the war? Perhaps that was why the other statues were being sought out. If there was information in them it could show that Mr. Sakura was an agent for the Japanese government. I wondered if Reverend Cecilia would not let me open the envelope.

Suzie's Return

My phone rang as I was having my morning coffee sitting out on my patio looking out over the valley and just enjoying the peace and quiet of my backyard. It is one of the reasons why I bought the place. The serene feeling I got from the view helps me to let go of all the stress I acquired over the many years of police work and now the private investigative business I started. I highly recommend it to everyone. Just then the tranquil nature of the moment was interrupted by my phone. Looking down I could see it was an unlisted number. I thought it might have to do with the case, so I answered it.

"Hello, this is Tom Sipowicz, how can I help you?"

I knew right away who it was when I heard the voice. "I'm guessing you're sitting on your patio looking out at the trees, am I right?"

"Yes, I am. But then again you pretty much know my routines don't you Suzie?"

"Pretty much, unless you've picked up some new ones since I was gone."

"So are you back to stay, partner?" I thought that might force her to give me an honest answer since she had always wanted to be my partner in the business.

"I'm not sure Tom, but I would like to meet with you to talk. It's still kind of early, perhaps you and I can get some dim sum. What do you think?"

"I would like that. Meet you at Li Wah in about an hour?"

"Sounds good. Oh, and by the way, my treat."

"See you there." I hung up the phone and went inside to get dressed. It wouldn't take me long to get to Asia Town and hell, I would never pass up free dim sum.

I arrived about ten minutes before Suzie and since it was a weekday they weren't too crowded. They seated me at my favorite table right by the kitchen so I could have first choice off the carts as they rolled out. The waiter brought me some tea and I poured a cup and wondered what Suzie had been up to since I saw her last. It had been several weeks since the shooting of her cousin and I hadn't heard from her at all after she disappeared. And right on cue she walked and headed straight for me. I got up to give her a hug and we both sat down to eat and talk. I could see in her eyes that she had something to tell me.

"I'm glad you agreed to meet with me, Tom. I know I owe you quite an apology for not letting you know what was going on with me after I left. But I needed some time to sort through some things."

"I understand Suzie, but I thought as partners we could help each other through any problems that we had, either professional or personal."

"I know but I was so distraught that I found myself out in California looking up an old friend from college. She and I were really tight, almost like sisters. I called her when I arrived and she let me stay with her and her husband. It was what I needed. I spent a lot of time on the beach just thinking and being alone with those thoughts."

"Did it help? Have you made a decision about whether or not you are coming back as my partner?"

"That's what I wanted to talk to you about."

I could sense from her tone that she was planning on leaving the business and giving up on our partnership. "Okay, let's talk."

"First, I want you to understand that I am very grateful to you for giving me the opportunity to be your partner. I'm not ending it at this point in time but I need to try something first."

So now I had mixed feelings about what she was saying. She's not ending the partnership as of yet but maybe in the future. What was the point she was trying to make? Did I still have a partner or not? "What is it you need to try and do?"

"My friend's husband runs a security business and he offered me a chance to try it out and see if I liked it.

If I did, he would hire me, and have me be one of his senior staff members."

"So have you come back to tell me you're staying in California?"

"No, I'm actually working right now. He gave me the opportunity to be the head security person for one of his clients who is here in Cleveland for an Import/Export symposium. I am his protection detail."

"Who is this guy that needs a security detail?"

"His name is Leo Greenwald and he runs an import/export business that has been in his family for many years. His grandfather started it before the Second World War and it is now in his hands."

"There are a lot of businessmen in charge of large companies and I don't know if they all have security details."

"He has a lot of friends in government and not just here but in other countries as well. If someone were to get their hands on him they could gather a lot of information and a big payout."

"So you've already taken the job then?"

"No, he let me do it on a trial run to see if I liked it and if I was a good fit for the company."

"How long is this trial period to last?"

"I'm here for a week with Mr. Greenwald and if it goes well then he will offer me the job and it will be up to me to decide if I want it or not."

My stomach sank as I began to wonder if she would like being in the security business more than being a private investigator. If she really liked doing it then I would be out a partner and more than likely lose a good friend. But I couldn't think about that at the moment. So I changed the subject to something a little less stressful and began to tell her about my latest case. I wasn't going to give her a lot of detail but just the overall gist of it.

We ate, filled up on tea and tried to make the meeting not so awkward. At the end she asked me if I wanted to meet the person she was working for as head of security. She was having dinner with him at his hotel, The Ritz Carlton in downtown Cleveland. She had already gotten permission from him to bring me along. She said she had talked me up to him and he was intrigued by some of the cases we had worked on and wanted to know if I would join them for dinner. I agreed to go, I mean after all, how often does one get to dine at the Ritz Carlton for free?

Meeting a Tycoon

Giving myself plenty of time I went home to get cleaned up and drove my car to the Van Aken Market District and parked my car by the rapid transit. I caught the transit down to Tower City which was right next to The Ritz Carlton. This way I didn't have to worry about finding a place to park and it was cheaper in the long run. I had a little time to spare so I went into the bar and had a quick drink and then headed to the lobby where Suzie said she would meet me.

I waited all of ten minutes when Suzie showed up and she was dressed to kill. Never had I seen her in such an elegant dress with all of the accessories to match. It was a black dress that came down to just below her knees and clung to her in a way that showed off her beautiful figure. A little clutch purse under her arm with what appeared to be a diamond bracelet on her wrist and earrings to match. She wore her hair in a way I had never seen before, she was stunning. I guess when you are in the field we are in you never really get a chance to dress up like this very often.

She walked over to me and said hello and grabbed me by the arm and walked me towards the restaurant where we were to meet her new boss. As we entered I could see a gentleman stand and raise his hand. He looked to be in his mid-fifties, with silver hair and dark blue suit. Just from looking at him I could tell he was fit and more than likely he went to the gym quite a bit. From my first glance I could tell he was the type of man who got whatever he wanted. Suzie angled me towards the table and as we neared it the man stood up to greet us.

"Hi Suzie, thank you for coming. And you must be the eminent Tom Sipowicz, aka, The Polish

Dragon. It's a pleasure to meet you sir."

"The pleasure is mine." As I shook his hand and waited for him to give me his name.

"Leo Greenwald." He said. "Please sit down." As he motioned towards the chairs.

Not wanting to be outdone, I held the chair for Suzie while she sat down. The way a gentleman would as I have seen many times in the movies.

"Would either of you care for a drink?" Leo asked.

Suzie said that she would have a glass of wine and I asked for a scotch neat. I don't really drink scotch but I figured, why not, if he's paying I might as well go all out. Who knew when I would get the opportunity again?

"So, Mr. Sipowicz, I understand that you have had quite the career as a private investigator. I would be very interested in hearing about some of your cases. Are there any in particular that stand out for you?"

"There have been a few but I wouldn't say they really stand out."

"Please share one or two of them with me please. If you don't mind?"

I proceeded to tell him about the case where the young man thought he was in communication with alien beings and how he went around the county kidnapping women, whom he thought would populate the new world that he was going to be taken to. He asked questions and I answered them for him.

Then I told him about Suzie's friend Andrew Sokolov who had the bible stolen and it turned out to be that his family was working for the CIA gathering information about Russia through his import/export business.

Again he seemed delighted to hear about the case but I had enough talking about my cases and wanted to know more about him, so I used the story as a lead into the next conversation.

"So I understand that you are in the import/export business as well, Leo. How did you get involved with that kind of business?"

Suzie gave me a glance which I had seen before from her. One that said how did you know that? But I managed to do my research before meeting him. When she asked me to meet her for dinner at the Ritz Carlton I assumed that she would be staying there as well as him. I found her name listed under the name of the corporation The Tutmondo Trading Company.

"Well my grandfather started the business in the early forties just before the United States got involved with the war because of the bombing of Pearl Harbor. He was taking trips to South America and Central America looking for things that Americans might want to buy for their homes. And after the war he was one of the first to obtain many items from Japan and China."

"How interesting. Did he have some sort of connection to be able to get into Japan and China right after the war?"

"I really couldn't tell you. Some of the things my grandfather did I am unaware of as was my father who has since retired and left me the business. My father was born in 1945 and I was born in 1967 and my grandfather had died when I was about ten, so I really didn't get to know him much."

My gut was telling me that something was not right with his story. I couldn't put my finger on it but it didn't seem right. He continued on about how the business grew and how he was here in Cleveland to give a talk at the Import/Export Symposium on Trade after the Pandemic. Then he asked a question that really got my attention.

"Do either of you know where I might be able to find a Buddhist Temple? I have been practicing for a while and would like to go and make an offering if possible."

Suzie thought nothing of it but I was really interested in why he became a Buddhist. Apparently his grandfather had imported some statues from Japan and China and as I boy he was really interested in them and when he went off to college he studied eastern religions and supposedly fell in love with Buddhism. I told him I knew of one and if he was interested I could take him there and show him the temple and he could make his offering if he so desired.

He seemed delighted that I knew of the place and we had made arrangements for me to pick him up in two days to take him to the temple before he headed home back to Los Angeles, where his business is located. Of course Suzie mentioned that she would be tagging along because it was part of her job as head of security to watch over Leo. She also wanted to go with me beforehand to check out the temple to make sure it was safe for her boss to visit. When I questioned her as to why, she informed me there had been threats against Leo and his family. Apparently, the person or persons said Leo would die exactly the way their family had died.

Suzie and I made arrangements to go the next day to the temple while Leo was giving his talk at the symposium. She would make sure that he was protected by two of the others she brought along just in case. Plus she knew the Cleveland Police would have officers on hand as well.

Visiting the Temple

The next morning I called Cecilia to make sure that it would be okay for Mr. Greenwald to come to the temple to pay his respects. She said it would be fine and that she would be there to let him in and to allow us to look around ahead of his visit. I made sure to tell her the reason was there had been threats on his life and Suzie wanted to make sure it was secure.

Suzie agreed to meet me at the temple, she would catch the rapid transit to the Van Aken District and just walk over to the temple. I agreed to drive her back to the hotel after we had finished securing the temple for Mr. Greenwald's visit. It was a beautiful sunny morning and I picked us up some coffee from the coffee shop in the marketplace at Van Aken. I waited for Suzie by the rapid stop where she would be getting off so we could walk together to the temple.

She arrived at the stop and smiled at me as she got out of the transit car and walked towards me. I handed her a cup of coffee and we began our walk to the temple.

"So how does it feel to be back in Cleveland?" I asked.

"It feels like I never left. Everything seems to be the same. Everything but me."

"Still haven't gotten over your cousin's death yet?"

"Not quite, but I have come to terms with the fact that he is dead. Still working on the fact that I was there and could do nothing to stop it."

"Suzie, it wasn't your fault. You would have done the same had he begun shooting at you. It was what we are taught in the academy. That split second timing between being alive or dead. The minute he shot he was destined to die."

"I understand all of that. But I feel like I failed him."

"Suzie he was in the cult for so long he bought into what Aaron was telling him. It would have taken years for him to be deprogrammed from that belief system. He might not even have been able to return to the person you once knew."

"I know, it's just hard to come to terms with it. Perhaps a change of scenery will help."

I could only interpret that as she was going to take the job as Greenwald's security chief and move to California. It made me sad because I was just getting used to her being my partner. Eventually I would have turned the business over to her when I felt like retiring from everything. She must have sensed my sadness and wanted to know about my new case.

I told her what I could about it and how it was proving difficult to find Hideki Sakura anywhere in the United States. And the fact that he more than likely died with his father in a fire at the internment camp Manzanar. She suggested what I already had thought of and that was to see if anyone who lived in the same barracks with them may know what truly happened. The problem was trying to find someone who was still alive that was there.

We arrived at the temple and Cecilia let us in and she showed Suzie around the entire building as she inspected every nook and cranny to make sure it would be safe for her boss to come and visit tomorrow. After feeling everything was in order and that no one else would be coming into the temple today, based on what Cecilia had told her, we left and I drove her back to her hotel so she could go and check on her boss at the convention center.

On the ride back to the hotel she told me about the threats that were being made to Mr. Greenwald and that they had started about a year ago. It was before she started as his head of security but she dove into all of the facts and threats that were made. The person or persons were very careful to not say much or leave any signs as to who they might be. You will die the way my family did, was all the threats said. Both on the phone and a few that were sent by mail. They assumed it was just someone who may have had a bad business deal with the company or someone with a mental problem.

The following day Suzie called to let me know they were headed for the temple, and I agreed to meet them there. I felt I could add some more security for her boss so that nothing would happen to him or Suzie. We arrived at the same time and they were in a limo that her boss must have rented while he was here for his visit. Suzie first scoured the area and then she and two others along with Mr. Greenwald headed to the door of the temple.

    Cecilia was there to greet us and take us into the temple where Mr. Greenwald could make his offering. He grabbed some incense sticks and lit them with one of the candles that was burning and bowed three times and put the incense into a cauldron in front of the Buddha statue. He then made a prayer and bowed three more times and asked Cecilia to show him around the temple. She obliged him and took him around the building with the security guards in tow. Suzie and I stayed behind to watch the door and make sure no one tried to get in.

"You have a beautiful temple here Reverend Cecilia, how many people are in your sangha?"

"We have about sixty people from all around the county as we are the only Shin Buddhist temple in Ohio. There are other temples but we teach Pure Land Buddhism founded by the Tendai Monk Shinran."

"Yes, I am familiar with that sect of Buddhism. I understand there are other temples around the country. Is that so?"

"Yes, some date as far back as 1933."

"When was your temple founded?"

"Our temple was founded in 1945 and we have been through several different locations before here. The original one was in the Hough area and was firebombed during the race riots in the sixties."

"Were you able to save anything?"

"Very few things were saved and whisked away by the original minister and taken to a house of one of the founding members. When we found a new temple, what was left was brought to the temple."

"I'm sorry to hear about that. If you by chance happen to need any more statues or Buddhist paraphernalia please, let me know. I have an import/export business and would be willing to get them for you at a reasonable price. Here is my card."

"I will do that and thank you so much for coming to the temple."

They walked back to where Suzie and I were staying and everyone said their goodbyes and we all left. I asked Cecilia if anything strange happened and she didn't recall anything other than the conversation about his business and the old temple. I left and headed home wondering what my next move would be to find the heir or heirs to the Sakura family. It was beginning to really bother me about what was in the envelope and if Reverend Cecilia was ever going to open and see what was inside.

A Strange Phone Call

Suzie was planning on heading back to California with her boss in a couple of days. He had some business meetings he had to attend and then wanted to see some of the Cleveland sights, like the Rock and Roll Hall of Fame, The Cleveland Museum of Art, and The USS Cod, a World War II submarine. I hoped I would get to see her one more time before she left but that would be up to her.

I settled in for the night, got myself a beer and headed for the patio to watch the sunset. It was a clear blue sky and the sun was just beginning to drop below the horizon and was shining its last bit of rays on the trees below my house. It was a peaceful feeling just taking it all in when I was startled by my phone. It was an unknown number and I debated whether to take the call or not. There had been a rash of those damn telemarketers trying to tell me my car warranty had expired but my intuition told me to take the call.

"Hello, this is Tom Sipowicz, what can I do for you?" Expecting to hear a recording from some warranty place I was shocked when I heard a person's voice.

"I understand that you are looking for my father, Mr. Sipowicz."

"That depends on who your father is." I said, knowing that I wasn't working on any missing person case other than the Hideki Sakura one.

"You are searching for Hideki Sakura are you not?"

I bolted up from my chair and stood staring out into the sun. Was this some sort of practical joke? If the Sakura family was burned in a fire in the internment camp then who could this possibly be? Someone from the temple perhaps trying to have some fun with me? "And who might you be?" I asked.

"My name is John Sakura and I understand that you are looking for my father."

"Yes, how do you know this and where can I find your father?"

"Why are you looking for him?"

"I have something that belongs to him. It's an envelope that was stuck inside of a Buddha statue at a Buddhist temple."

"Which temple?"

"The Cleveland Buddhist Temple in Shaker Heights."

"I will contact you again in a day or two. Look for a package to be delivered to you. Do not try to trace this call as the phone will be destroyed when I hang up. Goodbye Mr. Sipowicz."

He hung up before I could ask any more questions. What type of package was he going to send me? Where was his father? This could only mean that Hideki Sakura did not die in the fire at the camp? So who did? Was there somehow a mistake made as to the names of the family that died?

Just when I thought the night couldn't get any more bizarre my phone began to ring again. This time I could see it was Reverend Cecilia calling. What could she want at this hour?

"Hi Reverend Cecilia, what's up?"

"I just received a call from one of the temple members and she said that it appears someone has broken into the temple. She lives across the street from the temple in one of the apartment buildings and she said she saw a light on inside the building. Then she heard a crash and went across the street to see what was going on."

"Did she see anything?"

"No, she got scared when she heard the crash and ran back to her apartment to call the police. They came to the temple and found the back door had been broken and when they went inside they had found several of the statues had been broken. They called me and I got there as soon as I could. Who would do such a thing?"

"I don't know, Reverend. Did the police find anything that could give them information as to who it might have been?"

"They have some people going through now to check for fingerprints and things like that. I will let you know if I hear of anything."

Before I responded I began to think if I should tell her about my other phone call with the so-called son of Hideki Sakura. Could this have some sort of bearing on the temple being broken into tonight? It is strange I get the call and suddenly someone is breaking into the temple. But suddenly I remembered that she still had the envelope at the temple.

"Reverend Cecilia, is the envelope still where you had left it?"

"I don't know. Let me go check."

What seemed like an eternity, she finally came back to the phone and said, "The envelope was exactly where I left it, in my desk drawer, behind some of the letters I received from the National Headquarters in San Francisco."

"Take the letter home with you and I will call you tomorrow when I find out what is going on."

"What do you mean? Is there something that you're not telling me?"

"I will share what I find out with you tomorrow. Stay by your phone and don't go to the temple until you hear from me. I have a few contacts at the Shaker Heights police department that I will call and see what's what."

"Fine. But if there is something you know and you're not telling me I'm going to get upset."

"Right now, it is better you don't know. I promise I will tell you what I know as soon as I get some answers."

I hung up the phone and headed inside when it dawned on me that maybe there was something left in my mailbox. Heading out to the end of my driveway I began to wonder what was going on. Did the person who called me have something to do with the break in and the temple? Were they looking for the envelope? And if they were, how did they know about it? The only people who knew were Reverend Cecilia, myself and the elders from the temple. Wait, some of their children had brought them to the temple because they couldn't drive. Perhaps some of them were involved with the break in and this phone call. But why? Was there something they were trying to cover up? Maybe they knew that Matsumoto Sakura actually was a spy and they were trying to cover it up. The only way to be sure would be to get a look inside that envelope and see what was inside.

Nothing in the mailbox I headed back inside to try and get some sleep. Fat chance of that I thought, I knew my mind would be racing back and forth trying to figure out what the hell was going on. I finally fell asleep and the last time I looked at the clock it was three in the morning.

The Break In

The next morning I headed to my office to call Ed Murphy, my contact at the Shaker Heights Police Department. He was the lead detective on the case when my friend Roger was kidnapped a few years back. If there was any information about the break in at the temple he would probably know about it. The call went straight to voicemail and I left a message for him to call me as soon as he could. In the meantime I would have to see what else I could dig up about this Sakura family.

If the person who called me last night was the son of Hideki then there had to be a mistake at the internment camp where the family was sent to. I didn't want to contact my friend again because I'm sure he gave me all that he could and I didn't want to put him in a spot. Just in case I needed him again in the future. But there had to be someone who knew what was going on. Perhaps the person who told me about Matsumoto may know more than what he is telling.

I called Reverend Cecilia and asked if she would be able to contact Akito Egawa to see if he would be willing to talk to me again. It would have been nice if Seiichi Masamune was still alive because he was the one at the same camp as the Sakura family. But maybe he had shared more with Akito than Akito was willing to share. She agreed to contact him and get back to me when she heard from him. She also wanted to know if it was safe to go back to the temple. I told her I hadn't heard from my contact at the Shaker Heights Police Department and as soon as I did I would call her right away.

As I sat in my chair wondering what the hell was going on when my phone rang and I could see it was Detective Murphy calling back. "Hi Ed, how's it going?"

"Not too bad Tom, how about you? It's been a while hasn't it?"

"Yeah, I've been quite busy lately with a lot of different and bizarre cases. Which is why I'm calling you."

"Oh, I figured as much. I'm guessing you want to know what we found out about the break in at the temple on Warrensville Center Road?"

"Yeah, you guessed right. Do you have anything yet?"

"We have very little, there were no prints found at the scene. More than likely the thief wore gloves and was very careful to not leave anything behind. There was someone who was out back of the condo building next door and said they saw a person dressed in all black sneaking across the golf course and hopping the fence on the back side of the temple."

"Did the person get a look at the face?"

"No, apparently he was wearing a ski mask but the tenant said the person walked with a slight limp. Almost like the person had a permanent leg injury. Right now that's all we know."

"Do you think it would be safe for the temple to open and have their services?"

"We don't see a problem with it and if they want we can post a patrol car nearby to keep an eye on the place but we don't think the person will be back."

"Why do you say that?"

"Just a hunch. It seemed like the person was looking for something particular because nothing was really missing. Some of the statues had been moved but other than that nothing seemed wrong."

"Thanks Ed. If you hear anymore please let me know."

"Will do."

I called Reverend Cecilia and told her what Ed had told me and that she could go back to the temple and conduct her business as usual. She said she was still a bit nervous and I told her that I would make sure the temple was safe, even if I had to be there myself. I asked her if the envelope was safe and she told me it was in a very safe place but would not elaborate any more than that.

We discussed the statues being moved and whether or not the person could have been looking for the envelope. I wanted to know if there was anything special about the one that had been broken and she said it was one given to the temple by Matsumoto Sakura and it was signed on the bottom. I thanked her for the information and told her I would meet her at the temple as she was planning on going there to check on things.

Now I began to wonder if the person who broke in was looking for the statue where the envelope was found. The other statues had been moved and maybe he was looking for the signature of Sakura. Whatever was in the envelope was worth breaking and entering and according to the phone call I got last night Hideki Sakura was still alive.

If what was in the envelope had anything to do with spying for the Japanese during the war, I could only assume that the information would no longer be relevant as the war had been over for over seventy five years. Whatever was in it, someone was still looking for it. Then it dawned on me.

The other four temples where the ministers were killed also had statues from Sakura. What if the person back then is still the same person looking now? He would have to be an older gentleman since the first temple robbery and murder was back in 1965. That means if it is the same person they would have to be in their seventies now.

Or perhaps someone was hired to find the statues and look specifically for the envelope. But what was so important they would kill for it? Perhaps there was more than information in the envelope. What if there was money in it? Or perhaps a location where money could be found. No one would know until the envelope was opened and the contents revealed. And unfortunately that wasn't going to happen until we found Hideki.

A Small Package Arrives

The next day I headed for my office after doing my usual morning routines of working out and having breakfast before heading out. I parked my car and headed across the street to get a cup of coffee to sip on while I was searching the web again to find out what I could about the Sakura family. The sun was shining and it was a beautiful day, not a cloud in the sky, and I was debating whether or not to just go over to the park and take a walk along one of the trails. Something told me just to go to the office and get started.

I opened the door to the office and there at my feet was a small manila envelope with my name on it. Picking it up, I walked to my desk, set my coffee down and opened up the envelope. There was a group of papers clipped together titled The Sakura

Family. Flipping through it to get an idea of what it was, it appeared to be a biography of the Sakura family. Sitting down I began to read from the very beginning.

Matsumoto Sakura was born in Akita, Japan in 1892 and was descended from one of the early samurai families. He moved to the United States in 1917 to try and establish himself as a businessman and created a company which would bring in goods from Japan to sell to Americans and then sell American made goods back in Japan. He worked very hard to establish his business in the Los Angeles area. His business started out slowly but eventually he began to make money and expand his business.

In 1925 he married Chiyo Furukawa and in 1930 his first son was born Hideki and two years later a second son who he named Yoshi and three years after that a daughter who was named Akira. The family lived in the Boyle Heights area of Los Angeles and interracial community of people with different ethnic backgrounds. There were schools, churches and temples geared to the Japanese population.

Matsumotos business was headquartered at Terminal Island which is about a twenty six mile trip from his home in Boyle Heights. The store/warehouse was located on Nagoya Way right on the waterfront. It was easy for shipping and receiving the goods that he was importing and exporting. Beginning in the 1940 he took on a young man who graduated from Harvard University with a degree in business and wanted to learn about the import/export business. The young man's name was Roger Greenwald and his family was a very wealthy and well connected family in California.

After the attack on Pearl Harbor and in the early months of 1942 President Roosevelt authorized the U. S. Army to remove nearly 120,000 Japanese people from their homes and sent them to internment camps created by the military. Nearly two thirds of the Japanese people who were removed were American citizens. Matsumoto was not a citizen but his children were and they were sent to the Manzanar Camp in California.

The family was set up in one of the barracks where they lived until their deaths in a fire. What was not revealed was that the son Hideki was next door with the neighbors when the fire broke out. But before the fire broke out Hideki had heard a noise in the middle of the night and climbed up the wall to see what was going on where his family was staying. The walls never reached the top so he was able to see over the wall, what he saw was kept secret for fear he would be killed.

Hideki saw a soldier demanding something from his father and when he refused to give the soldier what he asked for the soldier stabbed him and the entire family. Unbeknownst to the soldier was that Hideki was next door and his family had taken in an orphan whose parents had died in the camp. To cover his crime the soldier then set the building on fire hoping that it would destroy anything linking him to the murders.

After the fire was raging he then began to yell about the fire but by the time anyone came to put it out the bodies were so badly burned that they couldn't be identified. Hideki, being with the family next door, told the husband what had happened and asked that he not reveal what he saw for fear he would be murdered. The father agreed and acted as if Hideki was his own son to protect the young boy. Hideki was only twelve years old and carried what he saw with him his whole life.

Now it is time for him to speak about what he saw nearly eighty years ago about how the U. S. Army had killed his parents and tried to cover it up. He is willing to speak with you Mr. Sipowicz, if you are interested in hearing the truth. You will receive a phone call with instructions on where and when to meet Mr. Sakura.

I couldn't believe what I had just read. Hideki Sakura was alive and he witnessed his parents being murdered back in the camp. But why had he waited so long to say anything? Why is he coming to me and what was it he wanted me to do? Why not just go to the authorities and tell them what happened? And when was this phone call going to come? I was now more confused than when I started this case.

But as I was wondering about all of this something suddenly caught my attention. Did it say that the person Matsumoto took on to train in his business was named Greenwald? Was this any relation to Leo Greenwald who happened to be in town for the symposium? I needed to contact Suzie to see if there was any relation between the two men.

The Greenwalds

I called Suzie immediately and told her that we had to meet. She wanted to know why and I told her that I couldn't tell her over the phone and I wanted to be able to meet her at the Ritz Carlton, where she and her boss were staying. Reluctantly she agreed but I could tell she wanted to know what was going on. I told her I would be there in roughly one hour and I would meet her in the bar.

I drove my car to the Van Aken District and hopped on a rapid transit car and headed down to the Ritz Carlton. When I arrived Suzie was already at the bar having a drink. I slowly walked towards her when out of the corner of my eye there was a man who seemed to be keeping an eye on her. Sitting down next to her I ordered a beer and she looked at me as if to say what the hell is going on. I took a sip of my beer and asked her, "Is Leo Greenwald any relation to Roger Greenwald?"

"Yes, that's his grandfather, why?"

"Let's just say that something new has come up in my case and I have a hunch that your boss has something to do with it."

"That's impossible. How could he? I've been keeping an eye on him since we got here."

"Not quite Suzie, you were with me the day we went to the temple to check it out and he was alone with some of his very personal bodyguards, right?"

"Yeah, so? They told me everything he did and everywhere that he went. They know they have to report to me as I am his head of security."

"If that's the case then why is there someone watching you? He's sitting at a table near the door."

"I know. I saw him when he came in. He's one of Leo's personal bodyguards. So what?"

"Well, why does he need to watch you if you're the head of security? Shouldn't he be standing guard outside of Leo's room?"

"I suppose, but I'm not going to question my boss. I'm sure there's a reason why he's here. Maybe he's just here for a drink like me."

"Take a walk with me, Suzie."

"To where?"

"What say we go across the street to the casino, and see if he follows you?"

"You're out of your mind Tom. Besides, we are getting ready to go back to California this evening and I need to make preparations."

"Come on Suzie, humor me. We'll take a quick trip to the casino and see if I'm right."

"Oh, yeah. I forgot about your legendary gut. Is your gut telling you something Tom? Or is this just your desperate way of trying to keep me here as your partner."

"Hey, listen if you want to go and be a security specialist by all means go. I won't stand in your way but if I'm right then your boss has something to do with the break in at the temple and perhaps his family is involved with several murders over the years."

"All right Tom." She said with anger in her voice. "Let's go to the casino and I'll show you that your gut isn't always right."

They got up and headed for the door as the man watching Suzie kept his eye on them the entire time. When they got to the street they hurriedly ran across and in the window Tom could see the man's reflection and he was tailing them. He also had a limp which made it hard for him to keep up.

Once inside Tom and Suzie headed to the escalator to the upstairs area where the gaming tables were and the high roller room behind that. They found a place out of sight of the gaming floor as they both watched the man limping around trying to find them. He was on his cell phone talking to someone.

"How long have you known him, Suzie?"

"Not very long, why?"

"Has he always had that limp?"

"Since I've known him. Why?

"Do you know what caused it?"

"No and I didn't ask, why?"

"A witness saw a man break into the temple the other night and the man had a limp. She couldn't make out his face but she knew he had a definite limp."

"So you think that this man broke into the temple? For what reason?"

"Let's just say maybe there is something that the Greenwald family doesn't want to be made public."

"Like what?"

"I think whatever is in that envelope may have something to do with the murder of a Japanese family in one of the internment camps."

She shook her head and began to walk away. I tried to stop her and she whirled around and began to lecture me about who the Greenwald family was. Starting with Leo. He had inherited the business from his father Bernard who had inherited it from his father Roger. She told me that the family was well connected back in California with many wealthy and political power brokers. Of course I knew this from the packet I received at my office.

Roger started the business and when the war was over he immediately began to bring in Japanese artifacts to sell in his business as well as sending American made artifacts over to Japan to be sold in a storefront he opened in Japan. He did so with the help of his political allies who bypassed much government red tape to allow him to set up his business there. He also was able to get many items supposedly from the Emperor's palace and was able to sell them back in California.

Bernard took over from his father and opened the business up to China, India and many Southeast Asian countries, which expanded it exponentially. Even when someone tried to compete with them the competitors always seemed to fail or were bought out by the Greenwalds, making them one of the largest import/export businesses in the world. At this point I realized that Suzie was beginning to get mad at me for even suggesting that Leo had something to do with the break in at the temple.

She headed towards the escalator and headed down and back to the Ritz Carlton. She didn't even say goodbye. Was I wrong for suspecting Leo and his bodyguard? Had I just ruined a partnership that I was hoping would get back together? Was my gut really wrong?

We would soon find out as I called detective Murphy in Shaker

Heights and told him what I had discovered and to see if it would be enough, maybe to hold the man for questioning and perhaps delay their trip back to California until I was able to find out more.

A Meeting with the Sakuras

As I began my walk back to Tower City to catch the rapid back to my car I received a phone call, again, from an unknown number. I assumed it might be Hideki's son, John, calling again. "Hello, this is Tom Sipowicz."

"Mr. Sipowicz, this is John Sakura calling."

"Yeah, I figured as much. What do you want?"

"There is a car waiting for you just outside the casino, please get in and they will take you to where you need to go."

I began to look around. How did he know I was at the casino? Was he following me? This case seemed to be getting more bizarre. Who was watching who?

"And where am I going?"

"You will see when you arrive Mr. Sipowicz. I suggest you hurry because the answers you seek are waiting for you."

I looked around and saw a black limousine parked across the street and the driver's window was down and I could see a man of Asian descent in the driver's seat and he was looking right at me. He nodded and I crossed the street to the car and he said, "Get in Mr. Sipwicz." I opened the back door and hopped in and there was nothing but tinted glass all the way around. I couldn't see the driver or where we were going. After about twenty minutes the car came to a stop and the door opened and I was escorted out by what appeared to be two body guards both Japanese.

There in front of me was a very large boat and I was at a Marina. From what I could see I knew I was at the Edgewater Marina because I could see downtown Cleveland in the distance. I was escorted aboard and taken below deck into a cabin where there sat an old Japanese man, who appeared to be in his late eighties or early nineties. The younger man sitting next to him appeared to be in his sixties and motioned me to sit down in a chair across from them.

"Mr. Sipwicz, I'm John Sakura and this is my father Hideki. We are pleased to meet you and we would like to welcome you aboard my father's boat. Would you care for anything to drink?"

"No, thank you. You can tell me why I was brought here in such a secretive manner."

"Of course. You were looking for my father and here he is. Now you can tell us why you were looking for him."

"First, why all the secrecy and the tinted windows, so I couldn't see where I was going?"

"Just a precaution Mr. Sipowicz. In case you haven't noticed you have been followed on multiple occasions. It appears that someone wants what you have or something you may know."

"The only thing I know is that there is an envelope with your father's name on it and it was hidden in a Buddha statue that apparently was made by your grandfather."

As I looked at the older man I could see his eyes brighten. Maybe he already knew what was in the envelope and maybe it was something I didn't want to know. I was beginning to feel like maybe I had wandered into a Japanese mafia problem and I was going to pay the price. The old man looked at his son and said something in Japanese and then they both looked at me. "Where is this envelope Mr. Sipowicz?"

"The minister of the temple has it and will not give it to anyone but your father. She wouldn't even let me open it to see what was in it. Do you have any idea what's in it? There seems to be someone else interested in this envelope because her temple was broken into a couple of days ago."

"What is her name?"

I gave him her name and then John had gotten up and left the cabin and I could see that two of the men that were there, probably bodyguards, followed him. He came back down and again asked me if I wanted anything to drink. I told him no and that I just wanted to get this case over with. I found Hideki Sakura and now my job was done and I just wanted to go home.

He told me I would be unable to leave at the moment and I would have to wait just a little bit longer before I could go. His idea of a little longer turned into two hours. As I sat there wondering what was going to happen and if I was going to meet my end at the hands of the Yakuza, Reverend Cecilia came down the steps into the cabin. I could see in her hand that she had the envelope with her.

She approached Hideki, bowed in front of him and handed him the envelope. Once opened I could see that whatever was written was in Kanji and I knew I would never be able to read it. Whatever it was, it was beyond me at this point. As I watched Hideki read with intensity and then handed the papers to his son, John. He then read it and a big smile came across his face. He thanked Reverend Cecilia for bringing the envelope and he thanked me for looking for his father so that she could deliver the envelope. I wondered if they would even share what it was.

The Delay

I and Reverend Cecilia were escorted off the boat and we were instructed to go back home and wait for a phone call when all would be revealed to both of us. John and his father had to leave momentarily and they would be back as soon as possible. Who knows how long that would take? As we headed for the limousine my phone rang and it was Detective Murphy calling. "What's up Ed?" I said. Hoping that he had some good news for me.

"I was able to arrest the man you mentioned as he was already at the airport with his boss waiting to catch a flight to California. He didn't seem to be upset and smiled pretty much all the way to the holding cell."

"Did he say anything to you?"

"Not yet but I am bringing in the woman who was the witness to see if perhaps she could make some sort of identification. It's a long shot but it's all we have right now. Were you able to get any more info?"

"Not quite sure yet. Things are still evolving as we speak."

"Well you better make it quick or you might lose your chance to close this case."

"Thanks Ed, I owe you one."

"That you do." He hung up and my phone rang immediately after that and I could tell it was probably Suzie. Although I didn't have her number I just had a hunch it was her.

"Hello Suzie."

"How did you know it was me?"

"Just a hunch, that's all."

"Oh yeah, you and your famous gut. Why has one of Mr. Greenwald's bodyguards been detained?"

"What makes you think I have the answer?"

"Listen Tom, I understand you are trying to solve a case but Mr. Greenwald and his people had nothing to do with it. So why don't you just let him go and we can head back to L.A. like we are supposed to?"

"I can't release him because I'm not holding him. He is a suspect in a break-in at the temple and the police are investigating him and having the witness go to the station to see if they can recall if it was him or not.

"Do you have some sort of vendetta against Mr. Greenwald? Or is this you getting back at me for leaving and quitting your company?"

"Suzie, I would never hold you back from anything you wanted to do, but remember you are still a detective unless you quit that job as well. And as a detective you know you have to follow all leads to see where it takes you."

"If you have any concrete proof about what is going on, then, I would be glad to listen to what you have to say."

"Well, I'm waiting for a phone call from Mr. Hideki Sakura and then, hopefully, I can give you some answers."

"Fine. I expect you to call me as soon as you hear anything."

"I will do that. Keep your phone handy."

With that we hung up and headed back to the temple to wait for Hideki's call. Both Reverend Cecilia and I were very curious to know what was written on the paper Hideki and his son read. My mind was thinking it had something to do with espionage and the good reverend didn't even want to venture a guess. Hopefully we will have answers soon and put this whole thing to rest.

The reverend made some tea and we sat in her office and waited for the phone call that we hoped would put an end to this ordeal. Neither one of us had much to say. I assumed we were both running things around in our heads to make sense of things. At one point she headed out to where she made her offerings and lit some incense and placed them in front of the Buddha statue. I really wasn't sure if that would help but then again, what could it hurt.

My phone rang startling us both and I could see it was Detective Murphy calling. "Hey Tom, just wanted to let you know that the witness is very confident the person in custody is the one she saw going to the temple. Unfortunately that is not enough to hold him and we are probably going to have to let him go. Unless of course you came up with some new evidence."

"Nothing at this point, Ed. I'm waiting for a call and hopefully all of our questions will be answered."

"I can hold him for a few more hours but then I'm going to have to cut him loose."

"I understand. Thanks, Ed."

A Meeting at the Temple

About five minutes after Ed hung up, my phone rang again. It was an unknown number but the way things were going I figured it had to be someone who was involved with this case and if I was lucky it might just be someone calling to see about my extended warranty. It would have been a nice break from all that was going on. "Hello, this is Tom Sipowicz."

"Mr. Sipowicz, this is John Sakura, my father and I are headed to the temple and we will meet you there in about an hour. Please be patient, it is just about over."

He hung up before I could even ask him what he meant by just about over. What was going to be over? As far as I was concerned my job was done. I found Hideki Sakura and the envelope was delivered to him, so it was finished for me. But what about the break in at the temple? Would that be over as well? Was Leo's bodyguard involved with that somehow or would he be cut loose for lack of proof? It would take about an hour before we would get any answers.

We had more tea and the good reverend told me some more about Jodo Shinshu and why she got involved with Buddhism and why she became a minister. She was born and raised as a Catholic as I was but she found that Buddhism suited her better. For me I went more towards the Daoist philosophy and the fact that we are all part of the same source and heading back to that very same source at some point.

Our discussion lasted almost a whole hour when she heard the bell ring at the back door. We both got up and headed for the door to see who it was, expecting it to be John and Hideki Sakura. Our mouths fell open when we saw that it was Leo Greenwald with Suzie at his side. By his car there stood at least three more bodyguards and who knows how many more were in the car or scattered around the outside of the temple. This did not bode well.

Reverend Cecilia opened the door and asked what they wanted. Suzie was the first to speak. "We received a phone call to meet here and that something very important was going to be revealed to us."

"Who called you?" I asked.

"It doesn't matter." Mr. Greenwald said with anger in his voice. "I should be on a plane back to Los Angeles but instead I'm here playing games with you people. My lawyers are going to sue the city of Shaker Heights for arresting my bodyguard and for harassment."

Reverend Cecilia invited them in and escorted them into the large open area where she performs her services. She made more tea and brought it out for everyone to drink and we all sat looking suspiciously at each other. I could see the anger in Suzie's eyes. It wasn't my fault that Leo's bodyguard fit the description of the man who broke in. It was strange that it happened while they were in town, so how was that my fault? Besides, I believe that she already had her mind made up to take the job and dissolve our partnership.

My mind began to wander, thinking about the cases that we worked on together and how we were great as a team. I really thought she was going to give up her position with the police department and join me full time. At least I had hoped that she would. The doorbell rang again bringing me back from my daydreaming. Again Cecilia and I headed for the door but I could also hear Suzie's footsteps behind us. When we got to the door, there stood John and Hideki was with him, only he was in a wheelchair. As like Mr. Greenwald there seemed to be plenty of bodyguards for them as well.

Now I really began to think that somehow or other I got myself involved with the Yakuza and something horrible was about to go down. But would they really do something inside of a temple? Would this be some sort of shootout and the victims would end up being me and Reverend Cecilia? Before my thoughts could go anywhere darker she opened the door, bowed to them, and escorted them into the area where we had all been waiting.

Both John and Leo stared at each, as if both of them knew what was going to happen. There was some tension in the air, and I could feel it. Suzie looked at me because she felt it too and we both wondered what was about to happen. John was the first to speak. "Please Mr. Greenwald, have a seat."

"What am I doing here? What is this all about?'

"It is about what your family has stolen from mine, Mr. Greenwald. And we demand restitution."

"Are you mad? Neither I nor my family has stolen anything from you. You must be out of your mind. I will not stay here and listen to this." He got up and headed for the door when John spoke.

"I have proof Mr. Greenwald, would you care to hear about it or have you forgotten all of the things that your grandfather and father had told you."

I could see in Leo's face that something hit home. He seemed scared and nervous. But the worst part is he never denied it. He seemed frozen in the spot he was standing in and again stated. "I have no idea what you are talking about."

"Why don't you have a seat then and I can explain everything to you. Or maybe you would prefer that it all comes out in the media. What would that do for your company and your image?"

Now everyone in the room began to stare at Leo wondering what he was going to do. It took him a while but he eventually went back to where he was sitting and sat down in the chair, waiting for the shoe to drop as they say. From what was just said I felt it was going to be a pretty big shoe.

The Assertion

As everyone was waiting attentively, John stood up behind his father and began to speak. "I'm going to tell a little story about how the Greenwald family became so successful and what they had done to become that way."

"This isn't necessary." Leo said. I could tell he was nervous because his voice was trembling slightly as he said it.

John continued on with his story. He talked about how his grandfather had arrived in the United States in the late 1800s, from his home in Akita, Japan, looking to start a business and make it rich in the United States. He managed to gather employment in areas of California, where the Chinese couldn't because of the Chinese Exclusion Act passed by Congress. The Japanese were able to go places that the Chinese couldn't. After several years of working in different jobs he was able to open a small store importing goods from Japan.

After a couple of years he was able to expand his business to exporting American goods back to Japan, which turned out to be a lucrative trading partner. Business became so good that he took on a recent graduate from the Harvard Business School, whose family was very well known in California. His name was Roger Greenwald. He became a valued member of my grandfather's business because he had learned things that would help the business grow. Plus, it didn't help having a connection with the well-to-do Greenwald family. They had connections in business, politics, and the banking industry.

When the war broke out my grandfather and his family had to be taken to an internment camp as most of the other Japanese families. But before he left he entered into a contract with Roger laying on the terms for the business. Roger would manage the business and change the name from Sakura Imports to a more Americanized name so that the business would not be taken away, as was the case with most Japanese businesses.

Roger agreed and when my grandfather returned he would make Roger an equal partner in the business. After the first year that my grandfather was in the camp, Roger decided that he wanted the business all for himself because he saw what a money maker it was. Even though he was unable to get merchandise from Japan he was still able to get it from South American and some of the Southeast Asian countries but those were mostly from the black market.

Knowing that he had signed the contract he now needed to find it and have it destroyed so that my grandfather would not be able to have the business back. But where could it be? He had no idea where the contract was and he assumed that my grandfather had taken it with him. With the help of his family he tried to get it back. His father, having connections with some politicians, managed to find which camp my grandfather had been taken to.

One of the guards at the camp was paid handsomely to find the contract among my grandfather's possessions. He was caught going through my grandfather's things when they awoke in the middle of the night and so the guard stabbed everyone and then set the building on fire.

"That's impossible." Leo said as he jumped to his feet.

He was standing right next to Suzie and she said, "Sit down and let him finish." At which he begrudgingly did.

John then continued on with his story. Unbeknownst to him my father Hideki was in the next cubicle over as he was staying with the family who had a son his age and they would often spend time together. My father saw what happened and did not say anything out of fear. Fear that no one would believe him and also that he might be killed. The only person he trusted was his friend's father who kept it a secret.

The guard never found the contract and then a short time later he was found dead outside of the camp fence. Apparently his failure did not go over well with the Greenwald family.

But what was not known was that my grandfather had put a note written in Japanese to my father and hid it in a Buddha statue which was given to several Buddhist temples. The note spelled out why it was hidden in the statue and where the contract was being kept.

The Greenwald family had somehow found out about the note in the statues and sent someone to find the note. That is how each of them was destroyed and the minister in charge of the temple murdered, just in case they may have known about the note. The only problem was the one in Cleveland. Everyone assumed the statue was destroyed in the fire that was set by the rioters during the Hough riots.

Once Leo found out it had not been found he sent someone to the temple to try and find it. But the statue had already been broken and the note protected by the Honorable Reverend Cecilia. Who in turn hired Mr. Sipowicz, to find my father and give him the note, which was rightfully his.

"You can't prove any of this." Leo shouted.

"But I can." John said and proceeded with the story. You see where your grandfather made a mistake was keeping many of the workers who my grandfather had hired and treated them with much respect and they reciprocated that respect. As they worked their way up in the company they had firsthand knowledge of what was going on. Roger had made sure that his son would do everything possible to find the contract and he passed that responsibility down to you, as he pointed at Leo.

Everything you and your family did to keep this secret was very well documented by those workers who were still loyal to my grandfather. They passed that responsibility down to their family members as well. So you see Mr. Leo Greenwald, my family should be half owners of Tutmondo Trading Corporation. We have the contract to prove it.

"You're lying. There is no way that you have the contract."

John held up an envelope to show Leo. Apparently the contract had been held in secret by one of my grandfather's most trusted friends. Who passed the responsibility of keeping the contract down to his children and grandchildren.

"So Mr. Greenwald, are you going to honor the contract or not?" John asked.

Leo jumped up and stormed out of the temple but before leaving he said, "You'll be hearing from my attorneys."

The Inevitable

As they walked out of the temple, Suzie turned and looked at me with confusion in her eyes. I could only imagine what she was thinking but I assumed that she was gone and I would never see her again unless she came back to Ohio to visit. Or if I ever decided to take a trip out to sunny California. I was sad to see her go but it was a choice she was willing to make.

John walked over to me to thank me for my help in locating the letter which told him where the contract was hidden and to help them answer some questions the Sakura family had for many years.

"Mr. Sipowicz, I would like to thank you for your help in locating the letter. Without you we might not have found it."

"No one else knew where it was at?"

"No. We knew it was in one of the statues and we assumed it was the one in Cleveland since nothing happened after the other ones were destroyed. It was assumed it was destroyed in the fire here in Cleveland and we lost all hope."

"You do realize that more than likely that will not hold up in a court of law?"

"Why do you say that?"

"Well, I'm no lawyer, but since both parties to the contract are dead I'm not sure you have much of a leg to stand on. It seems to me that no judge would take on a case like that. But I'll also bet you have some good lawyers on your side, who will make sure that one way or another the Greenwald family will pay."

"Yes, we do."

"May I ask you a question then?"

"Sure, what would you like to know?"

"How did your father make all of his money?"

"When my grandfather, grandmother and aunt and uncle were murdered, my dad went back to Japan after the war because he knew he could make a good living."

"Doing what?"

"My dad learned a lot about the construction trade here in America and when he went back to Japan he formed his own company and made millions of dollars off of rebuilding the cities."

"Why did he come back to America?"

"First he was an American citizen and second the Yakuza was starting to make headways into the construction businesses so he sold his business before that happened and left. Then when he returned here to the states he invested a lot of it in the stock market."

"Well it seems like everything will work out for you and your family then. Even if you don't get half of Tutmondo Trading Corporation."

"We're not worried about that Mr. Sipowicz. You see, my father has already looked into buying the controlling interest in the company. So if Mr. Greenwald does not honor the contract or even admit to the wrongs his family has done, he will still lose quite a bit."

Apparently, the Sakura family had everything planned out. My assumption now was that they wanted

Leo to admit to what his family had done and seek retribution for the murders of the family members. Not to mention the ministers at the other temples. Of course there is no statute of limitations on murder so maybe they can find the person or persons involved with their murders and bring them to justice.

As for the murder of Matsumoto Sakura and his family, the guard who killed them was brought to justice by being murdered himself. I will look forward to reading about a lot of this in the newspaper when the story breaks to see how the media twists everything around. I'm sure of it because of the Greenwald's deep pockets. They will try to buy the storyline and slant it towards them.

I headed home to relax after this case because it took its toll on me emotionally. Learning how badly the Japanese Americans were treated by their own government and the fact that I lost my partner in the business. Polish Dragon Investigations would have to find another partner or continue to go solo.

As I pulled into the driveway I could almost taste the beer that I was wanting to drink on my patio and look over the valley and wonder what the world was coming to. Once in the house I tossed the keys on the counter and headed for the kitchen to grab that beer. Something was not right, there was a breeze coming in from the patio door and as I whirled around I could see a figure sitting on my patio drinking one of my beers. I pulled my gun from the drawer where I keep it and headed slowly to the patio.

As I approached the door I heard a voice say, "Is that how you greet your partner, with a gun?"

It was Suzie and she looked at me, lifted her beer bottle and took a swig. "What are you doing here?" I asked.

"We're partners right? Don't partners drink together?"

"I thought you were heading back to California with Leo?"

"Nope, I can't work for a guy like that. Too much underhandedness for me. Besides, I like solving cases with you Tom."

"So, you've overcome your feelings about your cousin?"

"Yes, I know that I can't bring him back and it was his choice to stay with the cult. I just wish I could have done more. And after today I learned that I could do more by helping those who need it. Those who come to you for help. That is if you will have me as your partner?"

I lifted my beer and we clinked the bottles together and I said. "Welcome home partner."

*"**If** you enjoyed my book, it would be greatly appreciated if you left a review **so** others can receive the same benefits you have. Your review will help me see what is and isn't working **so** I can better serve you and all my other readers even more."*

Other Books by Steve Zimcosky

- The Old Man From the Hill (Lessons in Qigong and Tai Chi) Volumes 1-4
- The Kid Hypnotist
- The Eagle and The Dragon (A Reiki Tale)
- The Last Reiki Hunter
- My Cursed Heart
- Love, Movies and a Dragon?
- The Revelations at Black Corners
- The Venusians Among Us
- The Haunting of Smock Hill
- The Blood of The Nephilim
- The Disappearance of Marty McRory

- Death of a Bully (Polish Dragon P.I.)
- Polish Dragon P.I. (The Ark of Healers)
- Polish Dragon P. I. (The Lineage Sword)
- Polish Dragon P. I. (Midnight Cranes)
- Polish Dragon P. I. (The Good Book)
- Polish Dragon P. I. (Hanging Cloud)
- Polish Dragon P. I. (The Protectors of the Inner Sanctum

Made in the USA
Middletown, DE
12 June 2022